I'm Going

MW01143726

These levels are meant only as guides;
you and your child can best choose a book that's right.

UP TO 50 WORDS

Level 1: Kindergarten–Grade 1 . . . Ages 4–6
- word bank to highlight new words
- consistent placement of text to promote readability
- easy words and phrases
- simple sentences build to make simple stories
- art and design help new readers decode text

UP TO 100 WORDS

Level 2: Grade 1 . . . Ages 6–7
- word bank to highlight new words
- rhyming texts introduced
- more difficult words, but vocabulary is still limited
- longer sentences and longer stories
- designed for easy readability

UP TO 200 WORDS

Level 3: Grade 2 . . . Ages 7–8
- richer vocabulary of up to 200 different words
- varied sentence structure
- high-interest stories with longer plots
- designed to promote independent reading

MORE THAN 300 WORDS

Level 4: Grades 3 and up . . . Ages 8 and up
- richer vocabulary of more than 300 different words
- short chapters, multiple stories, or poems
- more complex plots for the newly independent reader
- emphasis on reading for meaning

LEVEL 3

Library of Congress Cataloging-in-Publication Data Available

2 4 6 8 10 9 7 5 3 1

Published by Sterling Publishing Co., Inc.
387 Park Avenue South, New York, NY 10016
Text copyright © 2006 by Harriet Ziefert Inc.
Illustrations copyright © 2006 by Tamara Petrosino
Distributed in Canada by Sterling Publishing
c/o Canadian Manda Group, 165 Dufferin Street
Toronto, Ontario, Canada M6K 3H6
Distributed in Great Britain and Europe by Chris Lloyd at Orca Book
Services, Stanley House, Fleets Lane, Poole BH15 3AJ, England
Distributed in Australia by Capricorn Link (Australia) Pty. Ltd.
P.O. Box 704, Windsor, NSW 2756, Australia

I'm Going To Read is a trademark of Sterling Publishing Co., Inc.

Sterling ISBN 13: 978-1-4027-3083-2
Sterling ISBN 10: 1-4027-3083-7

For information about custom editions, special sales, premium and
corporate purchases, please contact Sterling Special Sales
Department at 800-805-5489 or specialsales@sterlingpub.com.

NO PLAIN HAIR!

Pictures by Tamara Petrosino

Sterling Publishing Co., Inc.
New York

I'm Brenda Fitzsimmons
and it's not fair!
I can't spend a whole week
with one kind of hair.

My hair will be different
and new every day.
No plain hair for me
when I have my way!

On Monday my hair will
have hundreds of curls.

Oh, I'll be the envy
of all of the girls.

On Tuesday I'll have spikes
all over my head.

The bangs will be purple.
The sides will be red.

On Wednesday evening
when I get a shampoo,
I'll make a bird's nest—
a soapy hairdo!

Peter will laugh,
and Johnny will scowl.
They'll say their sister
looks like a stuffed owl.

If it's sunny on Thursday,
I'll make braids that are long.

I'll lean out my window
and sing a loud song.

A headband on Friday
will make my hair dressy.

When I go out,
it will never get messy.

For Saturday's boat ride,
I'll make ponytails.

I'll look quite terrific
while watching for whales.

On Saturday evening I'll keep very busy.
I'll try conditioner for hair that is frizzy.

I'll try spray shine and gloss,
gold dust and confetti.

I'll see how I look with
bangs of spaghetti!

I'll put on a crown
and say,

"Now you're
a queen."

Then I'll pull
my hair tight
and look terribly
MEAN!

I'll let my hair loose
and what will I see?
A girl smiling back
who looks just like me.

On Sunday I'll clean up my room,
then I'll call my friend Dee.
I'll spend the whole day
just being me!

No barrettes!

No bows!

No headband!

No confetti! No shine!

No gold dust!

No ponytail!

No braids!

But by Monday I'm bored
and my hair seems too plain.
I'll get Mom to braid it
like a show horse's mane!